This Walker book belongs to:

_____

_____

_____

For Emma and Tiffany

First published 1996 by Walker Books Ltd
87 Vauxhall Walk, London SE11 5HJ

This edition published 2008

10 9 8 7 6 5 4 3 2 1

The moral rights of the author and illustratorhave been asserted.

This book has been typeset in
ITC Garamond Book.

Printed in China

British Library Cataloguing
in Publication Data:
a catalogue record for this book
is available from the British Library.

ISBN 978-1-4063-0632-3

www.walkerbooks.co.uk

Once Upon a Picnic

Conceived and illustrated by John Prater
Text by Vivian French

WALKER BOOKS
AND SUBSIDIARIES

LONDON • BOSTON • SYDNEY • AUCKLAND

Out for a picnic
Mum, Dad and me.
Not much to do.
Not much to see.

Mum is setting
up the chairs.
Here come
the three bears.

Mum and Dad
just sit and dream.
Is that a troll
beside the stream?

Nothing much
for me to do.
Who's that little girl
talking to?

Now I'm hungry
what's in here?
Biscuits, apples,
ginger beer…

That kite's high
above the ground.
What's that giant
stamping sound?

Run! Run!
As fast as you can!
Run and play
you gingerbread man!

Mr Wolf is
by the trees.
That girl's flowers
made him sneeze!

Look! A witch!
Perhaps her spell
isn't working
very well.

All those children
in that shoe.
Look how much
they have to do!

We've been sitting
here all day…
Little bear
might like to play.

Playing ball
is so much fun.
Come back, come back,
everyone!

Another title by
John Prater

ISBN 978-1-4063-0633-0

Available from all good bookstores

www.walkerbooks.co.uk